The Bumblefly

Carolyn Hanna Crawford

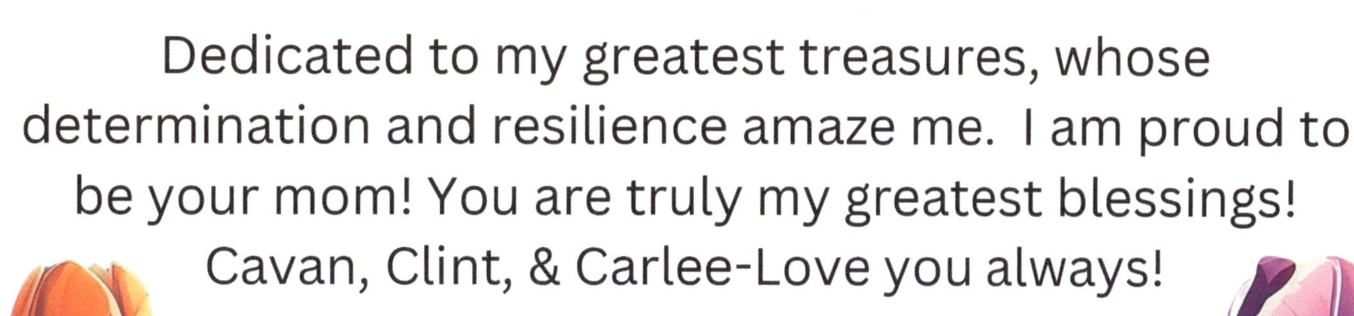

Dedicated to my greatest treasures, whose determination and resilience amaze me. I am proud to be your mom! You are truly my greatest blessings! Cavan, Clint, & Carlee-Love you always!

ABOUT THE AUTHOR

Carolyn Hanna Crawford grew up on a small rural farm, where she developed a deep appreciation for animals, nature, and the world around her. Now an experienced elementary school teacher, Carolyn brings her passion for positive storytelling to young readers. Her books reflect her love for the earth and her belief in kindness, aiming to inspire joy and thoughtful lessons. Carolyn is the proud mother of three and the grandmother of two.

In a meadow green, under a bright blue sky,

Lived a creature that could make
you wonder why.

With wings like a butterfly, fuzzy and grand.

It's the Bumblefly,
a marvelous sight to see.

Buzzing around with such joy
and glee.

With a buzz-buzz here and a flutter fly there.

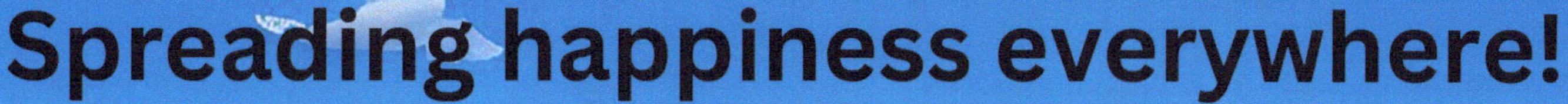

Spreading happiness everywhere!

With a fluffy body and
wings so wide.

She'd zip through the air with a bumblebee glide.

Collecting nectar from flowers
tall and small.

Spreading colors and cheer,
one and all!

In gardens and fields,
she'd dance and play.

Bringing smiles to creatures along her way.

For the Bumblefly knew,
as she flew by.

That spreading joy was the greatest high!

So if you spot her,
with wings so bright...

In the golden sunlight's warm delight.

Give a cheer, a wave,
or a happy cry.

For the wonderful creature,
the Bumblefly!

the
End